MW01045741

"I DIDN'T DO IT!"

CASEY WEST

Artesian **Press**

P.O. Box 355, Buena Park, CA 90621

STANDING TALL MYSTERY SERIES
MULTICULTURAL READERS
SET 3

Back From The Grave	1-58659-101-0
Cassette	1-58659-106-1
Guilt	1-58659-103-7
Cassette	1-58659-108-8
"I Didn't Do It!"	**1-58659-104-5**
Cassette	**1-58659-109-6**
Of Home and Heart	1-58659-105-3
Cassette	1-58659-110-X
Treasure in the Keys	1-58659-102-9
Cassette	1-58659-107-X

Project Editor: Molly Mraz
Illustrator: Fujiko
Graphic Design: Tony Amaro
©2003 Artesian Press

 Artesian **Press**

ISBN 1-58659-104-5

CONTENTS

Chapter 1 5

Chapter 2 14

Chapter 3 18

Chapter 4 26

Chapter 5 35

Chapter 6 41

Chapter 7 47

Chapter 8 55

Chapter 1

Alex yawned and stared at the clock. A sign that said "Come on in! We're Open" hung in the front window of Gator Movie Rentals, where Alex worked. He counted the seconds until he could flip the sign so that "Sorry, We're Closed" showed through the window. He hoped no last-minute customers would come in before then—that would keep him there at least another fifteen minutes. Most people took a long time to pick out a movie to rent.

The store was empty; it had been that way for the past hour. Outside, the moon made shadows on the concrete. It was almost ten o'clock, and Alex needed to get home and start his homework. He was supposed to read *Othello* by next week, and he hadn't even started.

Alex rubbed his eyes and yawned again. This job was great for extra cash, but it didn't leave him much time for homework or sleep.

Alex looked up at the clock again—ten o'clock.

"Yesssss!" he said aloud. "Sorry, folks, we are closed." He stepped out from behind the counter. He was halfway to the door when he saw a shadow stop outside. Alex held his breath and hoped whoever it was would just walk away— but the "Come on in! We're Open" sign was still out, and he knew this would probably make him lose an hour of sleep tonight.

The door opened, letting in a rush of damp air. It was September, but it still felt like August. In spite of the heat, Alex felt a chill when he saw the person who entered the store. Now he was sure he would lose an hour of sleep tonight. The shadow hadn't belonged to a customer but to Mr. Lowell, Alex's boss. Mr. Lowell loved to stop by just before closing to do "random checks," which took forever and served no real purpose other than to make the employees feel like criminals.

"Good evening, Alexandre," Mr. Lowell said. Alex frowned. He hated being called by his full name. It seemed like Mr. Lowell's way of reminding Alex that he was different, just because Alex was from Haiti.

"Hi, Mr. Lowell," Alex said. The moonlight made a shiny ring on Mr. Lowell's bald head. It made Alex want to laugh, but he didn't.

"And how is everything going tonight?" Mr. Lowell asked.

"Great," Alex said. He reached behind the counter and picked up his backpack. "I was just getting ready to lock up."

"Not so fast, young man," Mr. Lowell said. "I have chosen tonight for one of my random checks, and you can't leave until I'm finished." Mr. Lowell grinned.

He loved making his staff wait around while he searched every inch of the store for "any signs of bad behavior," but lately it seemed like Alex got more "random checks" than the other kids who worked there.

"Mr. Lowell, I've been working since four o'clock," Alex said. He tried to sound as respectful as possible. "I really have a lot of homework to do." Alex stepped toward the door, but Mr. Lowell blocked the doorway.

"It is your fault if you don't manage your time wisely, young man." Mr. Lowell said. He always spat when he talked, and Alex tried to stay out of his way. "I don't care what you have to do tonight. You are my employee, and you will wait until this random check is over."

Alex frowned. He hated Mr. Lowell.

"Well, let's get started," Mr. Lowell said, an evil look of joy on his face.

Alex looked at the clock and sighed. This was going to be a long night.

One hour later, Alex stepped outside into the sticky night air. He walked toward the parking lot, his face was hot with anger. Behind him, he heard Mr. Lowell come out of the store and lock up. Alex kept walking. His feet pounded on the pavement. He felt his heart pounding, too.

He reached the parking lot and his car—a beat-up green convertible. He loved that car. He worked all summer to save enough money to buy it, and it was the only reason he couldn't quit his job now. He needed money for his car insurance, and for gas. He enjoyed the independence that came with owning his own car, and he didn't want to give it up now.

Alex grabbed his keys out of his pocket and unlocked the door. He loved the way his car smelled, like cheeseburgers and deodorant. He threw his backpack into the passenger seat. He was getting into the driver's seat when someone poked him on the shoulder. Alex was so surprised, he fell down on the ground. Before he could look up to see who poked him, Alex heard a familiar laugh. It was his best friend, Ben.

"Ben," Alex said, "You scared me. What are you, a stalker?"

Ben laughed. "I prefer the term admirer."

"Yeah, go ahead and laugh at me," Alex said. He was laughing too, though. "How did you know I was still here?"

Ben wiped tears of laughter from his eyes and caught his breath. "I called your house, and your mom said you weren't home yet."

"Right," Alex said.

Ben reached out his hand and helped Alex to his feet. "Why are you so late?" Ben asked.

Alex didn't want to talk about it. "Get in," he said. He sat down in the driver's seat. "I'll drive you home."

Ben walked around the car and got in. "Let me guess," Ben said. "Was it another random check?" Ben said *random check* as if it were a product he was trying to sell on television.

"You guessed it," Alex said. He knew Ben was just trying to make him feel better, but he wasn't in the mood for jokes. He started the car and drove toward Ben's house. They drove in silence for a while, and then Alex turned on the radio.

"Why do you let him bother you?" Ben asked. He wasn't joking anymore.

"I don't know," Alex said. "I need the work."

"Come on, man," Ben said. "You don't need this. You could find another job."

"Yeah, right," Alex said. "Nobody hires teenagers for good jobs. It would be the same anywhere else."

"I don't know about that," Ben said.

"Plus, I need to pay for this little beauty," Alex said. He patted the dashboard.

"That reminds me," Ben said. "I've got a date with Tanya tomorrow night. Can I borrow your car?"

Alex turned the car into Ben's driveway. He sighed. "Aw, man, you know I don't like it when other people drive my car."

"Other people?" Ben said. He looked hurt.

"Sorry," Alex said. "It's been a long night." He paused. *Great—a Friday night with no car.* Oh well, Ben *was* his best friend. Besides, Alex knew he needed the car. Tanya, the girl Ben was dating, expected a lot. Her family had a lot of money, and she was used to being treated like a princess. While Alex's car wasn't exactly worthy of a *princess*, it was the closest Tanya was going to get if she dated Ben.

"Of course you can borrow the car," Alex said.

"Thanks," Ben said. He put out his hand, and Alex shook it.

"See you tomorrow," Alex said.

"Later," Ben said. He shut the door and walked up the driveway to his front door.

Alex watched until Ben was safely inside and then drove home. *Maybe,* Alex thought, *independence isn't so great.*

Chapter 2

Alex awoke to a sudden chill of cold air that went from his toes to the back of his neck. He grabbed for his blanket, but it was gone. He took the pillow from under him and slammed it on top of his head. His mom giggled.

"Mama," he said, his voice raspy. "Stop! Five more minutes."

"You've had five more minutes five times already, cupcake," he heard his mom say. Her voice sounded muffled to him underneath the pillow.

"Gimme back my blanket!" he said.

"Nope," his mom said in her usual cheerful voice. He growled. As if staying up until two in the morning doing his homework wasn't bad enough, now he had Miss Cheerful taking his blanket and calling him "cupcake."

"Get up, Cupcake," she said. "Grandma made *beignets*," she said.

He sat up and opened his eyes. A blurred image of his mom's face came into focus. "What time is it?" he asked.

"Time to get dressed," she said. She giggled and left the room.

Alex looked down and realized he was in his underwear. He jumped out of bed and pulled on a pair of jeans.

"Hasn't anyone ever heard of privacy in this house?" he yelled as he walked down the hallway to the bathroom. A wonderful smell led him toward the kitchen instead. He had missed dinner last night, and he was starving. *Well, at least Mom wasn't lying about the beignets.*

His grandma was in the kitchen making breakfast. Alex smiled. It had been only a few months since she'd come to the States from Haiti, and Alex loved having her there. Besides, she was a much better cook than his mom.

"Morning, Grandma," Alex said. He grabbed a plate from the cupboard and helped himself.

His grandma came over and gave him a quick kiss on the forehead. She always knew when he wasn't in the mood to talk.

His mom didn't. She came into the kitchen and began chattering. He loved her, but he wished she would stop talking every once in a while. Still, he felt bad for her. He knew that since his dad left, she had no other men to talk to.

"Up late again?" she asked.

"Yup," he said. He took a big bite of food to discourage any more talk, but that didn't stop her.

She poured coffee into an old brown mug until it spilled out over the sides. "You know," she said, "I think that job is going to hurt your grades if you aren't careful." She picked up the too-full mug, leaving a brown ring on the counter top. Grandma came behind her and wiped the ring away with a sponge.

"I'm being careful," Alex said. He took another bite.

"Marie, don't pester the boy," Alex's grandma said with her heavy accent.

His mom opened her mouth to say something, but just then, the phone rang. She answered it.

"Good morning, Ben," she said. "He's right here." She held the receiver out to Alex. "For you," she said. She took her coffee and left the kitchen.

"What's up?" Alex said, his mouth full of food.

"You going to pick me up for school?" Ben asked. Alex could tell he was eating breakfast, too.

"Sure. I'll be there in ten minutes," Alex said. He hung up the phone and gobbled down the rest of his food. "Thanks, Grandma," he called as he walked down the hall to his room and got ready for school.

Chapter 3

That day at school, Alex fell asleep in three of his classes. After school, he waited for Ben in the parking lot.

While he waited, he saw Janna, another Gator Movie Rentals employee, walking toward him. He leaned on the hood of his convertible with one elbow so she would know the car was his.

"Hey, Alex," she said.

"Hey, Janna."

"Cool car," she said.

Alex smiled. "Yeah," he said. "I paid for it with my huge Gator-guy salary."

She laughed. "How'd it go last night?" she asked.

Alex rolled his eyes. "Guess," he said.

"Uh-oh," she said. "Did you get

another random check?"

"Yep." He polished a spot on the hood of the car with the hem of his shirt.

"I don't know what he has against you," she said.

"I do," came a voice from behind them. It was Ben.

Alex's face felt hot. Ben always teased him about Janna.

"Okay, Ben," Janna said. "What does Mr. Lowell have against Alex?"

"He can't stand having an employee who is so handsome and strong," Ben said. He reached over and squeezed Alex's cheeks. "Just look at that face."

Janna laughed. "I've gotta go," she said. "See you later, guys."

When Janna was out of sight, Alex punched Ben lightly on the arm.

Ben laughed. "What was that for, man?"

"For making me look like a fool when I was trying to show off my car," Alex said.

"You still don't mind if I borrow it

tonight?" Ben asked.

"Naw," Alex said. "I'm going to catch up on my English project tonight anyway."

"Thanks," Ben said. "I think Tanya will appreciate that I don't have to drive my dad's car again."

Alex laughed. Ben's dad was a plumber, and his car had advertisements all over it. It was not what you would call a great date car—especially not to Tanya. He tossed the keys to Ben. "You drive," he said. "Drop me off at home, and you can take the car from there."

"Cool," Ben said.

They got into the car, and Ben started it up. The hum of the motor made Alex relax for the first time all day.

"So where are you gonna take Tanya tonight?" Alex asked. He rolled down the window.

Ben frowned. "I don't know," he said. "I was thinking Moe's Shrimp Shack."

"Does she like those kinds of places?"

Alex asked. He wanted to tell Ben to forget Tanya and find a girl who didn't care where he took her to dinner or what car he drove. He hated to see his best friend get treated this way, but he kept his mouth shut. He could tell Ben was embarrassed.

"I'm not sure," Ben said. He drove out of the school parking lot and turned onto Buchanan Street. "She likes pretty expensive stuff, I guess."

"Like how expensive?" Alex asked, though he probably could have guessed.

"Well," Alex said, "she wants me to take her to this stupid girl-music concert next month in South Beach, but the tickets are eighty dollars each."

"Ouch," Alex said.

"You're telling me," Ben said. He stared out at the road in front of him.

"Are you going to take her?" Alex asked.

"I want to," Ben said. "But where am I going to get that kind of money?"

"True," Alex said.

They dove past Gator Movie Rentals, and Ben laughed. "Hey, we could rob Gator Movie Rentals," he said. "I heard Marty from school made close to two hundred dollars selling used DVDs on the Internet."

"Yeah," Alex said. He laughed, too. "I would love to see the look on Mr. Lowell's face." He could just see Mr. Lowell's beady eyes open wide at the thought of all his precious DVDs, gone forever. They both laughed.

"This car is great," Ben said.

Alex nodded. "Just make sure you bring the car and the keys back tonight, though," he said. "I have to open the store tomorrow morning at eight-thirty."

"No problem. I'll come to your house after I drop Tanya off."

"You better, because I can't be late," Alex said. "If I have one more argument with Mr. Lowell, I think I'll scream."

"Then I hope for your sake there's no big robbery at the store tonight," Ben said.

He winked. "Because if there is, we both know who will have to go through another random check."

Alex laughed. "Yes, we do," he said.

Ben drove into Alex's driveway, and Alex got out. He shut the door and said good-bye through the open window.

"Take good care of my baby," Alex said, patting the hood of the car.

"I'll guard it as if it were my own!" Ben yelled as he drove away.

It was almost midnight when Ben tapped on Alex's window. Alex was asleep face down in his copy of *Othello* when Ben woke him. He could hear Ben's muffled voice through the glass.

"Let me in, man. I'm getting bitten by bugs out here."

Alex rubbed his eyes and took a deep breath. He chuckled to himself. Ben was like a mosquito magnet, and it seemed that every mosquito in Miami gathered in front of Alex's house. He opened the window, and Ben practically fell through.

"Well, it's about time," Ben said. He scratched at a reddening bump on his arm. "Were you asleep already?"

"Already?" Alex said. He pointed at his bedside clock. "It's midnight."

"Man, you need a little excitement in your life," Ben said. He grabbed a stuffed soccer ball from the floor and threw it at Alex.

"How was your date?" Alex asked. He tossed the soccer ball under his bed, embarrassed that his best friend saw a toy in his room. His grandmother brought it from Haiti for him.

"Cool," Ben said. He bit his thumbnail. "Tanya actually liked Moe's Shrimp Shack."

"Cool," Alex said. "You got my keys?"

Ben pulled the keys out of his pocket and gave them to Alex. "Here they are," he said. "Thanks again, man." Ben looked at the ground.

"Any time," Alex said. He plopped down onto his bed. He wanted to sleep.

Besides, Ben was acting strangely.

"So, are you, um, going to drive me home?" Ben asked.

"Okay," said Alex. He slipped on some sandals. "Let's go."

Chapter 4

The next morning when Alex drove into the parking lot of Gator Movie Rentals, there was a crowd gathered in front of the store. That was weird, because the store didn't open for thirty minutes. It was even weirder that two police cars were parked in the parking lot.

Alex pushed his way through the small crowd and into the store, which looked like a hurricane had hit it. He walked to the back of the store and was shocked to see that at least half of the DVDs were missing from the shelves. He heard a wheezy voice behind him.

"There he is."

Alex turned to see Mr. Lowell and two police officers walking toward him.

"Alexandre," Mr. Lowell said, "how nice of you to join us this morning."

"What do you mean?" Alex asked. "I'm not late."

"No, young man," Mr. Lowell said. "I'm just surprised you showed up for work at all, after your late night last night."

"What are you talking about?" Alex asked. He knew the two policemen were staring at him. "What happened here?"

"It will be easier if you just confess now and hand in the stolen merchandise," Mr. Lowell said. He took a step toward Alex.

Alex felt his face getting red. "What?" he yelled. "I never stole anything!"

"Oh no?" Mr. Lowell said. He seemed pleased that Alex was so upset. "Then how do you explain all the DVDs that disappeared from our shelves last night?"

"Why should I have to explain them?" Alex asked.

"Because," Mr. Lowell said, an evil

smile on his face, "you are the only student employee with a key to this store."

Alex stopped. Mr. Lowell was right. He *was* the only student who had a key, and that made him look like a thief. But he wasn't. He didn't even have his keys last night—Ben had them.

Alex suddenly had a terrible thought. Ben! At first he told himself no way—Ben wouldn't do something like that. Or would he? Alex needed to get out of the store fast and talk to Ben.

"I didn't even come here last night," he said. "I didn't steal anything."

One of the police officers walked to the front door and began looking closely at the lock. The other didn't say a word. Alex wondered if they thought he was guilty, too.

"Who did then, Mickey Mouse?" Mr. Lowell asked. "I suppose he got bored at Disney World and decided to steal our movies and have a party."

Alex wanted to slap the smile right off

Mr. Lowell's face, but he shoved his hands into his pockets instead.

Finally the police officer, who according to his name tag was Officer Jacobs, spoke. "Son," he said. His voice was kind. "Where were you last night?"

"At home studying," Alex said.

"Oh, please!" Mr. Lowell rolled his eyes. "On a Friday night?"

"Yeah," Alex said. "Is that a crime?"

Officer Jacobs cut in. "Can anyone prove that you were home?"

Alex shook his head. "I was home alone," he said. "My mom and grandma went to the movies."

"What about after they got home?" Officer Jacobs asked.

"They went to bed as soon as they got back," Alex said. He felt as though he had lost already.

"And you didn't leave the house at all?" Officer Jacobs asked.

Alex would have loved to tell Officer Jacobs that he gave Ben his keys and that maybe Ben was the one they should go question, but he hadn't talked to Ben yet, and he didn't feel right telling on his best friend. He needed to choose his answer very carefully. "I left only once to give my friend a ride home," he said. He quickly added, "He got dropped off at my house after a date."

Officer Jacobs raised his eyebrows. "And what time was that?" he asked.

Alex gulped. Did the officer know he was lying about how Ben got to his house? "Around midnight."

Mr. Lowell said, "Isn't that convenient? The police think the store was robbed between eleven and one."

"Look, I swear I didn't take anything," Alex said. "Why would I do that?"

Officer Jacobs put up a hand to silence Alex. "I'm sorry, son, but we would like to search your backpack and your car."

He didn't sound angry, but Alex could tell he was serious. Alex took off his backpack and held it out to Officer Jacobs.

Then he reached into his pocket and got out his keys.

Twenty minutes later, Alex drove into Ben's driveway. He'd been "released" from work until the stolen DVDs were returned. However, to Mr. Lowell's disappointment, the police said there wasn't enough evidence to charge Alex with the theft, even though he was the main suspect.

Alex slammed the car door and walked through the grass to Ben's window. He pounded on it so hard, he almost broke the glass. He could hear Ben fumbling toward the window. Then he saw the miniblinds open, showing thin slits of his friend's face.

"What's the deal?" Ben asked. "Why aren't you at work?"

"Come outside," Alex said. He turned and walked to the front door without waiting for a reply.

A few seconds later, the front door

opened. Ben walked out in his pajama bottoms and no shirt. His hair stuck up in back. Normally, Alex would have made fun of how he looked, but not today.

"Glad to see you were having such a nice sleep while I was getting fired!" Alex yelled.

Ben's eyes opened wide. "You got fired?"

"Don't do that, Ben," Alex said. "I know you stole the DVDs."

"What are you talking about?" Ben asked.

Alex took a step closer to Ben. "The store got robbed last night, and you had my keys." "You know I wouldn't do that," Ben said. He scratched a mosquito bite on his shoulder.

"Yes, you would," Alex said. "You said so yourself yesterday."

"I did not," Ben said. He stepped closer to Alex.

"Yes, you did," Alex said. "You said you could make some extra cash by robbing the store and selling the DVDs."

"Alex, what's the matter with you? I was kidding." Ben laughed nervously.

"Isn't that a coincidence?" Alex said, immediately sorry that he sounded so much like Mr. Lowell. "You need money to take your snobby girlfriend to a stupid concert, and suddenly two hundred DVDs disappear from the store on the night you have my keys."

"Stop being such a jerk!" Ben said. "You're supposed to be my best friend."

Alex rolled his eyes. "Gimme a break. You are hardly 'Best Friend of the Year,'" he said. "I'm going to lose my job if you don't return those DVDs."

Ben looked like his head was going to explode. "Alex, for the last time—I don't know where the DVDs are," he said. He turned and walked toward the front door. Before he went inside, he turned and shouted, "But if I did, there's no way I'd tell you!"

"Fine!" Alex yelled. He stomped back

to his car and got inside. He sighed and ran his fingers through his hair. "Fine."

Chapter 5

Alex sat on his bed, trying to figure out the events of the last twenty-four hours. He lost his job, his best friend, and his reputation all in one day. The hardest part was not having Ben to help him solve the problem. He couldn't believe Ben would do this to him. *Maybe it wasn't Ben*, he thought. *Maybe I'm just jumping to conclusions.*

He threw his pillow on the ground and lay down on the bed. It had to be Ben. Ben was the only one with a key. He needed the money, and he acted weird when he came to Alex's house to drop off the car. All the facts pointed to Ben, but Alex still felt bad for accusing him.

Alex needed to find those DVDs—and

the thief—before the police did decide to charge him with the crime. He needed proof, and he was determined to get it.

The next day, Alex walked down Charles Street, looking for clues. He passed Gator Movie Rentals. Through the front windows, he could see Janna with a customer. He paused. If he went inside, would everyone think he was there to steal something else? He didn't care—he needed to find out where those DVDs were. As soon as he walked inside, Janna came out from behind the counter and ran up to him.

"Are you okay?" she whispered. "I heard all about it."

Alex ran his fingers through his hair. "Yeah, well good news travels fast, I guess."

"Who do you think did it?" she asked.

Alex blinked. "You don't think I did it?"

"Of course not," Janna said. She put

her hand on his shoulder. "I knew the minute I heard that it must have been someone else."

Alex felt relieved that someone believed him, especially since that someone happened to be a very pretty girl.

"So, do you have any idea who did it?" Janna asked.

Alex looked around the store before he answered. He spoke quietly. "Well, to be honest, I accused Ben of taking them."

"Ben?" Janna asked. "But he's your best friend. He wouldn't do that."

"It seemed like he did," Alex said. He was suddenly very ashamed for accusing Ben. "But now I'm not so sure."

Janna walked over to the Action/Adventure section of the store, and Alex followed. "It's too bad this all happened now, with the store going out of business," Janna whispered. "It won't help things." She straightened the DVDs on the rack.

"What do you mean?" Alex asked.

Janna stared at him. "Didn't you know?" she asked. "Mr. Lowell is declaring bankruptcy next month."

"What?"

She hunched down behind a shelf and motioned for Alex to do the same. He did. Janna told him, "Mr. Lowell can't pay the store's bills."

"Are you sure?" Alex asked. His mind was racing all of a sudden.

Janna nodded. "Mr. Lowell told me himself," she said. "He said we should all look for new jobs before the store closes."

"Mr. Lowell never told me that," Alex said. His heart pounded.

"I wonder why," Janna said.

"I don't," Alex said. He got down lower, until he was almost sitting on the ground. "Janna, can you think of a way it would help someone to steal from his own store?"

Janna's eyes narrowed. "I'm not sure I understand you."

"Businesses have insurance to cover their losses," Alex said. "If an owner stole his own stuff and made it look like a thief did it, he could collect the insurance money."

Alex could see that Janna was thinking. "You don't think that . . . ?"

"Yes, I do," Alex said. "Janna, do you know what this means?"

"I think I do," she said. "But how can we prove it?"

Suddenly, proving that he was innocent wasn't the most important thing to Alex. "I'm not sure about that, but I do know I've made a huge mistake about Ben," he said. He rose to his feet and glanced around the store. A few customers were waiting in line.

"You better go make it right, then," Janna said. She got up and saw the line of customers. "Sorry," she called to them. "I'll be right with you."

"What time do you finish work?" Alex asked.

"Five," Janna said.

"Meet me at my house, okay?" Alex said. "We'll need your help."

Chapter 6

This was the second time in two days that Alex knocked on Ben's window, but this time Alex didn't pound. He stood outside the window for five minutes before he got the courage to tap lightly on the glass.

The window went up, and Alex saw Ben's face through the water-stained glass.

Ben opened the window an inch and spoke through the screen. "What do you want?"

"Can I talk to you?" Alex asked.

"What does it *look* like you're doing?" Ben said. He clearly wasn't going to come outside. "Go ahead and talk."

"Okay," Alex said. "I just wanted to tell you I'm sorry. I know now that you didn't steal the DVDs."

"Yeah?" Ben said. He rested his elbows on the windowsill.

"I was unfair, and I should have listened to you," Alex said. "I'm sorry."

Ben looked less angry, but he still wouldn't accept an apology that easily. "That was really mean of you," he said.

Alex sighed. "I know. I'm sorry," he said. "But why were you acting so weird when you came to my house Friday night?"

Ben picked at a spot of chipping paint on the windowsill. "Because Tanya broke up with me."

"What?" Alex said. He was relieved, but for his friend's sake, he needed to look surprised. "Why?

Ben looked up at him. "She hated Moe's Shrimp Shack," he said. "I was too embarrassed to tell you."

Alex couldn't help but laugh at the fact that Ben took the richest girl in school to a really crummy restaurant, and she broke up with him because of it.

Ben tried to hide his own laughter. "It's not funny."

"You're right, I'm sorry," Alex said, but they both still laughed.

"But seriously," Ben said, "what made you believe me anyway?"

Alex remembered that he was trying to solve a mystery. Now that he had his best friend back, there was work to be done. "I think Janna and I figured out who did it."

"You and Janna, huh?" Ben raised his eyebrows. "Way to go, my man."

"Never mind," Alex said. "I'm serious."

"All right," Ben said. "So, who done it, inspector?"

"I think it was Mr. Lowell," Alex said.

"What?" Ben asked.

"I don't have time to explain," Alex said. "We need proof."

"What's your plan?" Ben asked.

Alex, Janna, and Ben spent all evening in Alex's bedroom trying to come up with a plan. Trying to prove that Mr. Lowell stole the DVDs was harder than they thought.

Ben leaned against Alex's desk and stared at the ceiling. "Do you think he has them stored in a warehouse or something?"

Alex shook his head. "It's only two hundred DVDs," he said. "He could store them practically anywhere."

Janna walked back and forth across the room, snapping her fingers.

"Janna, stop," Alex said. "You're making me nervous."

Janna looked up at him. "Sorry," she said.

"Okay, let's think," Alex said. "Should we break into Mr. Lowell's office and find the insurance claims?"

"Nope," Ben said. "All those would prove is that he's trying to collect money for the DVDs you stole."

"Plus," Janna said, "even if we wanted to get in, I don't have a key, remember?" She started walking again.

"That's not a problem," Alex said. He pulled his keys out of his pocket. "I still have mine."

Janna stopped walking and grabbed the keys out of Alex's hand. "What?" She looked through them until she found the key that opened Gator Movie Rentals.

"Yeah, Mr. Lowell forgot to take my key," Alex said. "So what?"

Janna thought for a moment, and then her eyes opened wide. "Oh, no," she said. "We've got to get to the store now. Come on." She sat down on the floor and put on her tennis shoes.

"What's wrong?" Alex said. He put on his shoes, too, though he didn't know what was happening.

"Alex," Janna said. "Employers don't just forget to take the key back from a suspected thief."

Ben put on his sandals. "What are you

trying to say?" he asked.

Janna looked over her shoulder at Ben. "Mr. Lowell left him with a key on purpose."

"Why would he do that?" Ben asked.

Alex finished tying his shoes and stood up. He understood now what Janna meant. "Because he wants to steal *more* DVDs, and make it look like I did it," Alex said.

Janna nodded.

"If he took my key away, the police would know it wasn't me," Alex said.

"Exactly!" Janna said. She walked out through Alex's bedroom door, and Alex followed. Alex heard Ben behind him.

"I still don't get it," Ben said.

Alex kept walking. There was no time to waste. "Come on. We'll explain in the car," he said over his shoulder. "Now, where can we find a camera?"

Chapter 7

Alex and his two friends sat close together behind some bushes at the edge of the Gator Movie Rentals parking lot. It was after eleven o'clock, and Mr. Lowell hadn't shown up yet. If they were correct, Mr. Lowell was going to steal even more DVDs from the store, and he was going to blame Alex for it. Still, as they huddled there, hungry and uncomfortable in the sticky air, Alex wondered if their plan was good enough.

"Are you sure this will work?" he whispered to Janna. Sitting this close to Janna, even behind a prickly bush, was kind of exciting.

"I don't know," she said. "But it's the only plan we've got."

"Ouch!" Ben yelled, and the others jumped.

"What's wrong?" Alex asked.

"I got bit by a mosquito," Ben said. "How long do we have to wait here?"

Alex sat back down on the grass again. "The police said the burglary probably happened between eleven and one o'clock on Friday night," Alex said. "Let's hope Mr. Lowell is consistent."

Ben laughed. "After all the random checks you had to go through, I'm sure he is."

"Hey, the random checks," Alex said. "So that's why Mr. Lowell always gave me more than the other employees."

Janna nodded. "He's probably been planning this for a long time," she said.

Alex looked down at the grass. "I always wondered why I was the only student worker with a key." At first, Alex thought it was because Mr. Lowell trusted him more than the others. Now he realized it was just so Mr. Lowell could use him.

"I didn't wonder," Janna said. "I always thought it was because of how responsible you are."

"Me, too," Ben said. He grinned in the moonlight. "But I also thought it was because of how handsome you are." Ben fluttered his eyelashes like a girl in love.

"Shut up, Ben," Janna and Alex said together.

All three of them laughed.

"*Shhh,*" Alex whispered, and the others stopped laughing.

Headlights shone on the bushes they were hiding behind, and the three of them fell flat on the grass. Alex could hear Ben breathing heavily.

A van pulled into the parking lot. Alex heard the motor turn off and the van's door open. Footsteps crossed the pavement in front of them. A pair of feet stopped in front of the bushes where they hid.

Alex held his breath. He was scared,

but he needed to know who those feet belonged to. He looked up through the bushes and saw Mr. Lowell's face in the moonlight. Mr. Lowell dug in his pockets for his keys. He found the key that opened the front door of the store and stepped away from the bush.

Alex let out a sigh of relief. Both his friends did the same. Alex looked through the shrubs at the DVD store's front door. He watched as Mr. Lowell looked all around the empty street and then let himself into the store.

As quietly as possible, Alex reached into his pocket and pulled out his mom's cell phone. He dialed 911. He felt his heart pounding. A woman's voice answered after two rings.

"911 emergency."

"Yes," Alex said. His voice shook. "I'd like to report a robbery going on at Gator Movie Rentals on Charles Street."

"Are you in the building, sir?" the woman asked.

"No, I'm just outside, and I'm watching it happen right now," Alex said.

"Are you in any danger?" the woman asked.

"No, I'm hidden," Alex said. "But hurry." He hung up and turned off the cell phone.

Both his friends stared at him as if waiting for directions.

"Janna," Alex whispered. "You stay here and take pictures of Mr. Lowell carrying DVDs out."

Janna nodded. She grabbed the camera that was hanging around her neck and turned it on.

"Remember," Alex whispered, "No flash. We don't want him to know we're here."

Janna nodded again.

"Ben, we need to keep Mr. Lowell here in case the police don't get here in time," Alex said.

Ben nodded, and the two boys carefully stood up. They checked to make sure Mr. Lowell couldn't see them before creeping over to the van. They squatted down behind the hood of the van and waited.

Alex had no idea how they were going to stop Mr. Lowell from leaving. He hadn't thought that far ahead yet. He just hoped the police would show up in time.

About ten minutes later, Mr. Lowell retuned to the van with a huge box. The boys stayed down low as Mr. Lowell struggled to open the back of the van and pushed the big box inside. Mr. Lowell shut the van door quietly and went back inside.

This happened three more times. Mr. Lowell packed three more boxes in the van and went inside for more.

"Wow, he's emptying the place out," Ben whispered after the store's front door swung shut.

Alex was getting nervous. Where were the police? His legs ached from squatting behind the van.

Mr. Lowell came out of the store, but this time, he put the box he carried down on the sidewalk. He pulled out his keys and locked the store's front door.

"This is it," Alex whispered. "He's leaving."

"What are we going to do?" Ben said.

"Stay here," Alex said. He knew what he had to do.

He stepped out from behind the car into plain view. Ben hissed at him to stay back, but he walked toward Mr. Lowell anyway.

Mr. Lowell was halfway to the van when he saw Alex. He dropped the box he was carrying, spilling DVDs all over the parking lot.

"What are you—how did you . . . ?" Mr. Lowell said. The nasty voice Alex knew so well was gone, and in its place was the voice of a frightened man.

"How could you do this to me?" Alex said.

"Do what?" Mr. Lowell asked, starting

to sound like he always did. "I've done nothing."

"I know you stole the DVDs and blamed it on me," Alex said. "And the police know too. They're on their way right now."

Mr. Lowell looked shocked. "How could a stupid kid like you figure something like that out?" Mr. Lowell could barely speak.

"I guess I'm not as stupid as you think," Alex said. He took a step toward Mr. Lowell.

"You can't do this to me," Mr. Lowell said angrily. He grabbed Alex and threw him to the ground.

Alex's head hit the pavement. The moon above him looked blurred, and Alex could feel Mr. Lowell's hands around his neck. The last thing he heard before passing out was the scream of police sirens.

Chapter 8

"Cupcake?" Alex heard. The voice sounded foggy and then became clearer. It was his mom.

"Cupcake, wake up," his mom said. She sounded very worried.

He opened his eyes slowly. He was still in the parking lot of Gator Movie Rentals. His head hurt terribly. He tried to sit up, but he was too dizzy. His mom put her hands on his shoulders.

"Don't move, Cupcake," his mom said. "They're bringing an ambulance."

"Mom," Alex said. "It was Mr. Lowell. He stole the DVDs and he…"

"We know all that, son," Alex heard another voice say. It was Officer Jacobs. "Your friends told us everything." Officer

Jacobs called them over, and Janna and Ben stood next to him, too. Now that his eyes were open, he could see a large circle of people gathered around him. His grandma was there, too.

"Mr. Lowell is being charged with the theft," Officer Jacobs said. "We want to congratulate you for your bravery."

Alex looked up into the faces of his family and friends. All of them looked so proud. He smiled, even though his head throbbed. "I'm just glad this is over," he said. "Now I can finally relax."

"Isn't your *Othello* test tomorrow?" Ben asked.

Alex groaned. "Maybe I can just watch the movie," he said.